Why do I feel bad?

Written by Susannah Reed

Illustrated by Ángeles Peinador

Collins

Who's in this book?

Listen and say

Download the audio at www.collins.co.uk/839733

Jill

Peter

Mark

🎧 Mia and Zac are at home.
Mia isn't happy.

Zac asks, "Are you OK, Mia?"
Mia says, "No. Why do I feel bad?"

Some days we don't feel good.
We feel bad.

May's friends aren't at school today.
She's sad.

Some days we feel angry.
Peter is playing with trains.

Mark can't play with the trains.
He's angry.

Some days we feel afraid.
There's a spider in the bathroom.

Jill doesn't like spiders.
She's afraid of them.

Feeling bad isn't nice.
What can we do?

We can talk to people. And we can
help our friends.

We can share our toys.

Or we can close our eyes and count to ten.

We can play in the playground or in the park.

We can play sports or we can ride our bikes.

We can draw a picture and we can learn about things.

Jill is drawing a spider and reading about them!

This is a small spider.

We can eat good food and get lots of sleep.

Mia says, "I'd like some food! Let's have lunch!"
Zac says, "OK."

Picture dictionary

Listen and repeat

afraid

angry

feel

happy

sad

share

1 Look and match

We can close our eyes.

We can eat good food.

Jill doesn't like spiders.

He's angry.

2 Listen and say

Collins

Published by Collins
An imprint of HarperCollins*Publishers*
Westerhill Road
Bishopbriggs
Glasgow
G64 2QT

HarperCollins*Publishers*
1st Floor, Watermarque Building
Ringsend Road
Dublin 4
Ireland

William Collins' dream of knowledge for all began with the publication of his first book in 1819.

A self-educated mill worker, he not only enriched millions of lives, but also founded a flourishing publishing house. Today, staying true to this spirit, Collins books are packed with inspiration, innovation and practical expertise. They place you at the centre of a world of possibility and give you exactly what you need to explore it.

© HarperCollins*Publishers* Limited 2020

10 9 8 7 6 5 4 3 2

ISBN 978-0-00-839733-3

Collins® and COBUILD® are registered trademarks of HarperCollins*Publishers* Limited

www.collins.co.uk/elt

British Library Cataloguing in Publication Data

A catalogue record for this publication is available from the British Library.

Author: Susannah Reed
Illustrator: Ángeles Peinador (Beehive)
Series editor: Rebecca Adlard
Commissioning editor: Zoë Clarke
Publishing manager: Lisa Todd
Product managers: Jennifer Hall and Caroline Green
In-house editor: Alma Puts Keren
Project manager: Emily Hooton
Editor: Barbara MacKay
Proofreaders: Natalie Murray and Michael Lamb
Cover designer: Kevin Robbins
Typesetter: 2Hoots Publishing Services Ltd
Audio produced by id audio, London
Reading guide author: Emma Wilkinson
Production controller: Rachel Weaver
Printed and bound by: GPS Group, Slovenia

MIX
Paper from
responsible sources
FSC™ C007454

This book is produced from independently certified FSC™ paper to ensure responsible forest management.

For more information visit: **www.harpercollins.co.uk/green**

Download the audio for this book and a reading guide for parents and teachers at www.collins.co.uk/839733